THE SMILE FACTORY
Copyright © 2018 by Todd Keisling
Illustration © 2018 by Luke Spooner
ISBN: 978-0-9830019-8-0
First NECON Chapbook Edition: July 2018

Cover design by Todd Keisling
Author photo by Erica Keisling

PRECIPICE

Published by Precipice Books | Womelsdorf, PA

www.precipicebooks.com

ALSO BY TODD KEISLING

A Life Transparent
The Liminal Man
The Final Reconciliation
Ugly Little Things: Collected Horrors

AUTHOR'S NOTE

Hell is a prison of metaphors. This one is mine.

THE SMILE FACTORY

TODD KEISLING

1
WE DON'T TALK ABOUT MARTY GODOT

You did a bad thing just now, friend. Never, *ever* ask about Marty Godot, especially when you're in earshot of management. I know you're new here, but believe me when I tell you, they have zero tolerance about this. I know there's nothing about it in the handbook, but just—yeah, I know, it's your first day, but for Boid's sake, *just shut up and listen to me,* okay?

Don't go by all that kumbaya horseshit they told you at your on-boarding meeting this morning. They gave you that speech to feed the illusion that they care about your well-being. Newsflash, friend: they don't, they never have, and they never will. And they certainly won't take kindly to you asking about the boogeyman, first day or not.

First thing's first: Yeah, I can tell you about him, but only this once, and only so you'll stop asking. That's the quick way to a promotion, and believe me, kid, that's the last thing you want. So, calm down, shut up, and listen.

You're probably wondering if I knew him, if I was there when he took off the mask, and the answer is no. I only know what I've heard.

Just like you. Just like everyone else here at ███████████. Sure, upper management and the drones in Human Resources did everything they could to squash the stories and keep Godot from becoming a martyr, but for all their brainwashing and cross-breeding, we're still somewhat human. Some of us, anyway. And what's more human than telling a story, spreading a rumor, or sharing gossip?

No, I didn't know him personally. I saw him every day, though, but that doesn't mean much. Working at the front desk here in the lobby, I see everybody, but I never spoke to him. Some employees have claimed to know him, but they're all lying. Everyone who knew him, worked with him, had anything to do with him on a corporate level or otherwise, is gone. And I don't mean gone as in "they resigned" or "their positions were terminated." No, I mean they were *promoted*. One minute they're in the cube next door, toiling away, doing their part to grease the company's gears; the next, they're missing from the daily motivation meeting, their nameplate on their cubicle is blank, and their name is scrubbed from the office email server.

Promoted. Assimilated. Digested into the greater corporate entity we know as the Benefactors. They've all gone on to become links in the great corporate chain, serving a higher purpose—which is what's going to happen to us if they catch us having this little chat, so listen up, and listen well. I'm only going to say this once.

You wanted to know about Marty Godot. Fine. Here's what I can tell you.

2
MONDAY MORNING MASQUERADE

The eyes of our Benefactors opened at dawn, draping the world in a warm reddish glow, and Marty Godot once again found himself standing in the lobby of ███████████. He couldn't remember how he got there, nor could he remember going home the night before; like every morning after the Acquisition, he found the concept of home was altogether foreign and unsettling, a bad dream of endless hallways and unreachable exits. In Marty's mind, there was only his time on the clock at the company, cushioned by the murky haze of nothingness in between, and the comfort of that routine filled him with a sense of purpose, a sense of place.

That place was among the other employees who filled the lobby's cavernous interior, already wearing their masks to hide the gradual desiccation, a grim side effect of this new reality. *The Monday morning Masquerade,* he thought. Marty found he was wearing his smiler mask, even though he could not remember putting it on—nor could he remember ever taking it off, for that matter. The smiler mask had always been a part of him, just like the rest of his dusty uniform of slacks, shirt, and tie.

As he followed his coworkers into a single-file line toward the security checkpoint, a stray thought wormed its way to the forefront of his mind: *What time did I leave last night?*

Marty thought about asking the young woman in front of him but paused when he noticed she was dressed in a black robe. Human Resources. Marty held his tongue.

The wrinkled guard with bleeding eyes offered a curt nod as he passed through the turnstile.

"Morning," Marty said. The guard said nothing, nor could he. His mouth was sewn shut, had been years ago during the Acquisition. He regarded Marty with pale blue eyes that wept red tears. *Morning,* those eyes said, *please kill me.*

Instead, Marty returned the old man's nod, and went on his way. That stray thought from moments ago followed, though, plodding along behind him like a lost dog, and Marty was none the wiser. Not yet.

3
MISERY MACHINES: A PRIMER

Something most people don't understand is that a day at the Smile Factory isn't respite from the agony of living. Sure, from the outside, working at the place where Euphoria™ is made must seem like the best thing ever. Take it from me, though, things aren't better on the inside.

Out there, you've got the madness of living beneath the unending gaze of the Benefactors. In here, you've got the misery of *working* beneath the unending gaze of the Benefactors. Two sides of reality, friend, and neither one of them's better than the other. Living brings madness brings mortality; working brings immortality brings misery. That's the cycle. Get used to it.

Once Charles Boid communed with them and the Acquisition began, most folks couldn't deal with the madness and started offing themselves. That's where we come in. We make the Euphoria™ to keep the lifers outside these walls sedated and happy in their insanity so the Benefactors can feed.

Where's the Euphoria™ come from? Misery, of course. *Our* misery.

What, you thought working here freed you from the suffering of living out there? You think they call it the Smile Factory because everyone in here's happy? Don't be naïve, kid. We're all wearing masks to cover up what this place does to us. You, you're fresh off the street, your soul's still mostly intact. Give yourself a few years, after the drain of the Benefactors starts to take its toll and go look in the mirror. I'll bet you one whole week's worth of Euphoria™ that you won't take the mask off ever again.

Sure, we make the happiness, but the Benefactors use our misery to do it. We're the misery machines that keep this Smile Factory running, and we've been given life to feed the maw of time.

Got it? Good. I'm doing you a favor by explaining. Marty had to figure it all out on his own.

4

THE BLEEDS

What time did I leave last night? Did I leave? How long have I been here?

Marty was so lost in the tumult of thoughts rolling around in his skull that he didn't hear Allan's voice carry through the cubicle wall.

How long have I been here?

"—Marty?"

"Yeah?"

"Did you see the email?"

Marty's computer chimed, signaling the arrival of a message. A bold subject line read: MESSAGE TO ALL ███████ EMPLOYEES. He opened the email and scanned the text, feeling his gut drop as he read the opening announcement about annual performance evaluations. The email began with "It's that time of year again!" and ended with "Best of luck! Boid be praised!" and for two seconds Marty felt the urge to put his face through the screen out of sheer frustration. Another year? That time again? When was the last time? And why can't he remember?

A creeping numbness seeped into his belly, filling him with a cold sweet nothing. His vision blurred for a moment like bad tracking on a VHS cassette, something he vaguely remembered but couldn't say why or when or where, and within moments he couldn't remember why he was so upset. There was only the hum of static in his head, a dull ache behind his eyes on par with any other day at the Smile Factory, and the slow crawl of warmth seeping down his cheeks.

Allan spoke up from beyond the void of Marty's cubicle domain: "Did you see it?"

"Yeah." Marty wiped the tears from his face and blinked away the mental dissonance. He skimmed the email again. "I wonder if we'll be chosen this time."

Allan peeked over the cubicle wall far enough to reveal the smile on his mask, a sentiment betrayed by the blood in his eyes. The dissonant juxtaposition of expressions put Marty in mind of a wounded soldier, shell-shocked beyond comprehension, just like what he saw on the news the first few nights after the Acquisition. The face of madness, so numb to the war happening around him that he'd accept any plight no matter what. Marty wondered if he looked the same but felt foolish for thinking so. Of course he did. They all did.

"You think it's true about the promotions?" Allan's mask caught the edge of the cube wall, knocking the smiling façade to the side, offering Marty a glimpse of the dried husk of flesh beneath. The desiccation always began with the mouth, the gums, the teeth. The soft parts. "I mean, they say you get moved on to something else, something better. Closer to the Benefactors."

"I don't know." Marty turned away, swallowing back the taste of phlegm in his throat. "Your eyes are bleeding again."

Allan blinked, and the red droplets pooling along the rim of his eyelids streaked down his cheeks beyond the rim of his facemask.

"You're supposed to take breaks," Marty said. "In fact, I'm due for mine in a few minutes."

"I know, I know…" Allan blinked again. "Go take your break. I'll catch you later. I need to deal with this."

Allan's half-masked face vanished behind the cubicle wall, and Marty took his cue to get up, stretch his legs.

In the employee breakroom, he found a group of ladies from customer service whispering to themselves, and Marty overheard "What if we're chosen?" and "Never heard from again" and "Got a promotion."

He'd heard these sentiments before, but he couldn't remember how many times or when, and it was this realization that invited the troubling questions back into his mind. How long had he been there? How long had he worked for ███████████?

There was a timeline in his mind—the time before the Acquisition, and the time after Charles Boid's communion—but the duration was beyond him. Measurable time had escaped him, torn away like scraps of cloth, and Marty found he couldn't escape the feeling that a piece of his mind was missing. Maybe the only piece that mattered.

"Marty?" One of the ladies in customer service pointed to him. "Sweetie, your eyes are bleeding."

He dabbed his cheek and his fingers came away crimson. Nodding, Marty mumbled "Thanks" as he fled to the restroom.

The bleeds were a part of the Acquisition, a side effect of the new reality mankind had to accept once the Benefactors took power. No one, least of all Marty Godot, understood the way everything worked, or why. What the Benefactors brought to this plane of existence was beyond human understanding. Only Charles Boid had glimpsed their true nature, linking their existence with ours through the digital domain. The Acquisition began shortly after, and… nothing. The rest was a blank canvas.

As he washed his eyes and cheeks, Marty realized he couldn't remember how much time had passed since that day. Years, maybe, but he couldn't remember how many. That question was another link in a chain of the morning's tacit queries, one more piece of a grand human mural wiped clean without a trace. One piece of many. How long had he been with the company? Did he leave the building last night?

All Marty remembered was his work: answering phones from screaming people outside the company while staring at a screen filled with the language of the Benefactors and deciphering their multi-tongued lingo into a dialect that human ears could comprehend. And before the job, before All-Father Boid's communion with the Benefactors, Marty remembered a life on the outside.

Those happier moments were so surreal and foreign that he suspected they might be fiction, another side effect from the Benefactors' influence on existence. A subconscious gag reel cooked up by his mind to make himself feel better while awash in all this misery. Before those sweet, almost idyllic memories, there was nothing. Another blank spot in Marty's mental mural.

There were only memories of happiness and the company, the Acquisition, the Benefactors. There was only his purpose within the corporate machine of ████████████. His department used to be known as Customer Transactions, but since the Acquisition, they were rebranded as Customer Transitions.

His role: Corporate Customer Transition Specialist.

His job: Deciphering the language of the sacred texts, fielding calls of the damned from outside the company, and fulfilling their orders for more Euphoria™. He had health benefits and a good 401(k), and someday, he hoped to retire—except those were pre-Acquisition sentiments. As an employee of the new corporate entity, Marty had no need for health insurance or a retirement fund. His oath of employment entitled him to benefits such as immortality and an eternity of servitude to All-Father Boid and their glorious Benefactors. Marty was a company man, had been for some time, and his life was devoted to the prosperity of ████████████, Boid be praised.

He stood at the sink with his hands under the lukewarm water. More red droplets slid down his cheeks and disappeared beyond the edge of his mask. A goofy grin of sickening happiness stared back at him in the mirror, accented with the sunken bloody eyes of a man who hasn't slept.

You're happy, that mask told him. *You're a part of something bigger. You're important. You matter.*

And Marty Godot, ever the company man, wanted so badly to believe in that smile. But as he left the restroom and returned to his desk, the incessant questions worked deeper into his fragmented brain like splinters he couldn't extract: *How long have I been here?*

———◈———

5
TAPEWORM TERMINALS AND YOU: A GUIDE

Your time at the Smile Factory will differ depending on your position, but regardless of your title, all positions serve the same purpose: to feed the corporate entity. Maybe you're one of the bean-counters in Finance, or maybe you're like Marty and doomed to suffer in Customer Transitions for all eternity. No matter what, you'll be hooked up to a terminal—here, it looks like this.

Handsome, isn't it? Looks like a giant tapeworm, yeah? Don't let its limp nature fool you. This fleshy appendage has hooked teeth, and while it may not look like much now, when you put it up to your skin it's going to wake up and latch on. Yeah, that's right. While you're working, it's hooked up to your arm or your thigh, maybe one of your legs, sucking out your life.

No, don't ask me about the science of it. "Science" died as a concept the day of the Acquisition. The Benefactors make things work by their will, and if this is how they want to drain us, who are we to argue? All things serve the company—even the worms.

So, when you take your seat and fire up your computer, you'll sign in by latching on one of these tapeworms. Me, I prefer to let it nuzzle just below the love handle. After a few days, you won't even know it's there.

That's all there is to it, really. You work, and it feeds on you.

Oh, the misery? Well, that's part of your existence now as an employee of ██████████.

Outside these walls, as the Benefactors complete the merger between their plane of torment and ours, the lifers are subject to the madness that comes with witnessing the impossible. I'm talking about the eyes in the sky as large as planets, large enough to have their own gravity, with dilating pupils like the red spot on Jupiter. The cyclopean structures sprouting from the earth, dripping with ooze and all non-Euclidean, riddled with glyphs that make your eyes hurt when you stare at them.

Within these walls, we exist on a different plane, and to exist here is to be steeped in misery. That burning feeling on your skin? The throbbing pressure behind your eyes? Or the anxious racing of your heart, like it might just burst from your chest? Yeah, that's all part of your life now. I wasn't kidding when I said we're misery machines. Simply being here hurts, sure, but at least you have job security.

The terminal tapeworms are just the collection method. Everything's connected to a central collection unit that runs through the building. Every terminal tapeworm is hooked into the Gut down on the production floor. Our misery gets sucked out, travels through the network into the Gut, and gets processed on the assembly line. There, the magical machines our Benefactors brought into existence from their plane of torment take the human misery and transform it into pure bliss. Euphoria™ gets packaged and transferred to the loading bays.

And from there, it goes out to every insane human on the planet.

Chin up, kid. Your suffering is going to help everyone beyond these walls remain docile and accept their fate. It's the American way.

6
YOUR CALL IS IMPORTANT TO US

"Your phone was ringing."

Allan's voice sounded like it was full of cotton. Marty ignored him, picked up the phone, and dialed his voicemail.

The message played back. A woman's cracked, desperate voice filled the line, a sound Marty's heard many times before. Her voice was a sound so achingly familiar and painful that, for an instant, reignited a passion deep down to reach out and help. But such moments were rare and fleeting, the passion snuffed out as quickly as it burned bright in the pit of his withering soul. By his estimate, Marty received between fifty and seventy-five calls a day, all of them from people screaming for help, for understanding, for an explanation. Between fifty and seventy-five times a day, another piece of Marty's soul would dry up, wither, and die.

Marty felt nothing as he listened to her plight. The woman's frantic, crazed expulsions of guttural noise numbed his ears, and he sat unfazed while her message played on for the better part of five minutes. The nature of her call was like all the others, related to the Acquisition and the arrival of the Benefactors, but her message cut off before she got to the point. Marty deleted the message and hung up, knowing she'd call back. They always do.

"Hey Allan," Marty said, reclining in his seat. Elsewhere, the sound of click-clacking keyboards and the low lurching gulps of the parasitic terminals filled the air over the cubicle farm. Someone screamed from a few rows over, followed by the clatter of a phone to the floor. *Promoted,* Marty thought, absently wiping a tear of blood from his cheek while a series of cryptograms flashed across his monitor. Another phone rang just a few cubes away, snapping him back to reality, and he cleared his throat. "Do you remember how long you've worked here?"

Allan's fingers paused on his keyboard, and the absence of the tap-tapping made Marty feel uneasy. *The absence of something,* he wondered, thinking back to the troubling gaps in his memory. *If I only notice when it's gone, was it ever really there to begin with?*

"I…well, sure. Don't you?"

"I don't. How long?"

"A while. A long time, I think, but—" Allan's phone rang. "Hold that thought."

But Marty didn't bother, because he knew Allan would be on the phone for a while. He could hear the muffled conversation leaking through the wall, overpowering the slow gulp of his terminal tapeworm.

"Thank you for calling ███████████. Your call is important to us. This is Allan speaking. How may I help you?"

Their script was tailored to address most customer concerns, especially during times of crisis, although the Benefactors urged employees not to refer to the Acquisition as such. According to Human Resources, referring to something as a "crisis" inferred negativity, and the Acquisition was anything but negative for mankind.

"Sir," Allan said, "sir, I understand your concern, but at this moment in time our glorious Benefactors have not authorized me to comment on that topic. Yes, I do understand and sympathize with the suffering you may be experiencing right now. Our Benefactors would like for me to remind you that such agony is trivial in the grand scheme of things, and if you would only submit to their will by following the recommended dosage of Euphoria™, your pain will—there's no call for such language, sir. I see. Uh huh. In that case, I must ask for you to submit your complaint in writing to our legal department—"

Marty listened, feeling something like pride in the way his coworker handled his call. Marty trained Allan long ago, but how long he cannot say, and the realization of his temporal dissonance dredges more unsettling emotions from the depths of his soul. He was about to disengage his phone's silent function and return from his break when an email with a subject line reading "Quick Meeting" arrived in his inbox.

He skimmed the body of the email twice, feeling his gut twist itself into tight knots. His boss wanted to meet with him about a performance review.

Numb, Marty Godot wiped a bloody tear from his eye and rose to meet his fate.

7
MANAGEMENT AND THE GREAT FOOD CHAIN

Once upon a time, maybe the greater entity of ███████ cared about the souls within its walls, but that all changed when the Benefactors took over. New initiatives were put into place. The company was restructured, reorganized to suit the needs of the business. Some were promoted to management, handpicked by All-Father Boid to be his cabinet of directors, and they remain at his side to this day.

Others were promoted as well, but to middle tiers to suit some frivolous purpose, often to stoke their teams into increasing output of misery, meeting monthly quotas, and so on. Those managers—the ones who embraced the ideals of the Benefactors, anyway—were the absolute worst.

Here's the thing about managers, supervisors, directors, or anyone else higher up the food chain than you and me. They're not human. I mean, sure, after what's being done to us, maybe we aren't exactly human ourselves—but that's more than what your boss can say, or his boss's boss, or their boss. My point is, the closer you get to the Benefactors, the less human you become.

Maybe it's a sudden loss of weight. Maybe it's a rash or cluster of pulsing boils on your skin. Most likely, it's the separation of your pupils like egg yolks. You start seeing the world differently, like they do. Reality loosens, stretches, becomes malleable in ways you didn't know was possible. The nature of the Benefactors begins to make sense somehow. And it wears you out. Your body can't take it. Neither can your mind. But you won't care, because you want to be closer to them. You want to keep climbing that food chain.

And that's what they want, kid. For you to strive to be more like them and less like you. Sure, you'll never *be* one of them, but the illusion is there so you'll try to be. That's their trap and it works every time. The more you try, the more misery you'll generate, because it goes against human nature to be so dead inside. Here at ███████████, down is up and up is down; the higher you climb the food chain, the more likely you are to be consumed.

8

SHORT-TERM PAIN, LONG-TERM GAIN

"Go-dot," Steve said, his shifting eyes alight with feigned excitement. He lifted his scrawny frame out of his seat and held out his hand. Marty closed the door, performed the bow as dictated by the new employee handbook, and took Steve's hand in his own. He pressed his lips against the manager's knuckles.

"Glory be to All-Father Boid."

"Glory be to Boid," Marty murmured, waiting for his superior to return to his seat. With the greeting ritual complete, Marty stared across the chasm of Steve's desk and tried to ignore the ball of bloody worms writhing across its surface. Steve flashed a wry sideways smile as he absently plucked a handful of the squirming flesh and tucked it into his mouth.

Marty watched his manager eat, unsure if Steve's choice of diet was the source of his unease, or if the absence of his smiling mask had something to do with it.

Management didn't wear the smiler masks like the rest of the employees, primarily because they wanted to show off their sacrifices like a badge of honor. His manager's face was gaunt, the man's skin stretched paper thin over bone, and his mouth was rimmed with the puckered wrinkles and scars of someone who'd worn their mask for years, maybe even decades. All that was left was a fleshy hole in the man's scarecrow face, his shredded lips pulled back and frozen in a repulsive scowl. Steve didn't need the mask anymore. There was no need.

"Working lunch?"

Steve grunted, slurping a wriggling pink worm between his thin lips. "Always. How are you, Mr. Go-dot?"

For a moment, Marty recalled a simpler time when such questions were genuine, but then he remembered his place and shoved the troubling memory back into the shadows.

"It's Godot, sir." Marty pronounced his name slowly—*guh-dough*—even though his effort was futile. Every meeting with his superior transpired with a reminder of pronunciation, and how many times had that been? Marty couldn't remember.

His manager nodded. A writhing, eyeless worm freed itself from Steve's shredded maw and flopped to the desk below. "Of course. I'm sorry. I'll make a note to remember next time."

Before the acquisition, Marty would've fallen for such sincerity. The lifeless, congealed stare of Steve's separating pupils and permanent scowl betrayed such a persona, and Marty knew better. Happiness and sincerity were not luxuries afforded by any manner of upper management.

Steve placed both hands on his desk, leaned forward, and whispered, "I have news from the Benefactors."

He muttered one of their names, and Marty's ears filled with a warm fluid that dribbled down his cheeks. Steve's head convulsed when he spoke the name, his throat swelling, the utterance of such awful sounds engaging a gag reflex so violent that his eyes nearly burst from his skull. His bluish-black tongue darted from his mouth like a dark tentacle, a slimy thing riddled with bulbous pox that shuddered and deflated with each pained syllable.

Seconds later, Steve's tentacle-tongue retreated to the fractured cavern of his mouth, and he regained his composure. "Where was I?"

"News from the Benefactors, sir."

"Yes." Steve sat up and adjusted his tie. The tie's fabric was wrinkled and stained, patterned with a repeating print of cartoon sheep, and Marty noticed one of the bloody worms attempting its escape in the shadow of Steve's collar. "The stars have aligned once more, ushering in a new season of performance reviews and possible promotions. I'm proud to say that you have been selected for review this year."

Marty felt the blood drain from his face. He opened his mouth to speak but found his words were frozen to his tongue. His mind wandered back to the women in the break room and their whispered gossip.

"I must say your transition numbers have improved, and your efforts have not gone unnoticed. You should feel proud. I know I do."

"Thank you, sir."

Steve cocked his head and cast a sideways stare at his employee. "You *do* feel proud, don't you?"

"Of course, sir. Incredibly proud." Marty's eyes began to bleed but he resisted the urge to wipe them clean. "Filled to the brim with joy. Glory be to Boid, glory be to the Many."

"Glory be to the Many." Steve closes his eyes in a quick pause of reverence before handing Marty a tissue. "Do you know why your eyes bleed?"

Marty took the tissue and wiped blood from his eyes. He did know, but he knew better than to steal his manager's thunder. "No, sir. Please tell me."

"Because you are unworthy to behold the glory of our wondrous Benefactors. Your ears are unworthy of hearing their names. Only through misery can you know salvation. Only through promotion will you become worthy. Our prophet Charles Boid foretold of it." Steve's pupils detached from themselves and floated independently, orbiting one another in the universe of his deadened eyes. "Your review will be painful, and it will be transcendent. But it's like I've always told you: Short-term pain, long-term gain. A synergy of give and take, for the Benefactors are righteous and fair. You will suffer for the greater good of the company, and your suffering will feed the Many."

Marty nodded. "Yes, sir. Glory be to the Many, glory be to Boid."

"Glory be to Boid." Steve turned away from his desk and toward the office window. Outside, the unblinking eyes of the Benefactors cast their gaze upon the earth, tinting the landscape in ruby red. Lightning arced along the horizon from beneath a roiling cloudbank. "Go, then, my child. The bishops in Human Resources are expecting you. It's been a pleasure working with you."

As Marty rose to leave, Steve found the worm hiding beneath his collar and popped it into his mouth. He nodded to Marty while he ground the invertebrate's soft flesh between his teeth. *Short-term pain*, Marty thought, closing the door behind him. *I wonder if the worm shared that sentiment.*

9
CORPORATE CUL~~TURE~~

Don't look an HR rep in the eye. Don't engage in idle conversation. You know what? It's better if you just avoid them altogether. You'll know them by the robes they wear, marked with the symbol of the Benefactors. All these altars around the office? They're set up to honor the sacrifice of Saint Newmarth, the former head of HR. That's why we're required to light a candle every time we pass one.

Anyway, here's the most important thing you need to remember about HR. They aren't like you and me. They aren't like your manager or anyone else who was promoted. The people in HR aren't people at all. You, you were born somewhere, maybe before the Acquisition but probably not. You had a life, hopes, dreams, all those juicy things that are slowly being sucked out of you on a daily basis. The people in HR weren't born at all. They were grown.

I've never seen the growing vats personally, but I've heard they're somewhere in the bowels of the facility. They say there's a place where the walls stop being walls, and start being layers of flesh that sweat and breathe. That's where the HR reps are grown and conditioned.

A common misconception about the Human Resources department, especially in the days prior to the Acquisition, was regarding its purpose. Many ████████ employees once believed HR existed to protect their interests, facilitating dialogue between the lower ranks and upper management and ensuring that the company's culture was friendly, inviting, fair, and productive.

The Benefactors corrected this mistake during the Acquisition.

The robed figures you might see wandering the hallways of the office, paying reverence at each shrine to Saint Newmarth, were created to enforce the will of the Benefactors. That is their only purpose. They worship at the altar of the company and will do everything in their power to protect its interests. Me and you, we're just assets. The human resources that keep this corporate engine running. And they're here to keep us in line.

So, don't talk to them. Don't look them in the eye. If you see them coming, turn the other way. If they ever want to meet with you, say goodbye to your coworkers, because the odds are not in your favor, friend.

And for the love of Boid, don't call them the Eldritch Gestapo.

10
SEEN AND UNSEEN

Marty wandered down the hall from Steve's office, his mind still reeling from the meeting. His gut was locked in an icy grip, twisting in upon itself, and he felt the urge to vomit. He'd never been selected for review before, and if HR wanted to meet with him, that could only mean one thing: *Promotion.* What had he done to deserve this?

The answer was obvious. Steve had even told him. His transition numbers were up and his efforts hadn't gone unnoticed. This realization was enough to send Marty's nausea into overdrive. He stepped into an empty cubicle at the end of the row and vomited into the trash can. A mound of squirming red things plopped into the bottom of the bin, and Marty turned away in disgust.

He'd broken one of the greatest unspoken rules of the company, whispered among his fellow low-ranking coworkers like heretic gospel: *Always leave room for improvement. Never do a great job.*

But he'd done a great job. What else was there to do but attempt to excel? Hadn't they told him that was his purpose? Aid the uninitiated as much as possible and help them transition into this new reality. That was his purpose, his mission, his *job.* And he'd done it well—but now he was being punished for it.

Steve's voice echoed in his head amidst the tumultuous noise: *You do feel proud, don't you?*

The lie had slipped from his tongue so easily. *Of course, sir. Incredibly proud.* Only that wasn't true at all. Admitting the lie went against all the conditioning in his mind and body, effectively undoing the investment the Benefactors had made in him when he took on the job however long ago.

Committing to the lie was something else altogether, something unheard of in the walls of ███████. A sin against Boid and the Benefactors was heresy, the punishment so severe that the employee handbook simply said "Don't do this" in its list of infractions and repercussions. Pressure rose in his chest and held him steady in its grip. Colors swam before Marty's bleeding eyes and he struggled to breathe.

Something's wrong. Something's wrong. I can't breathe. I can't—how long have I been here? Where did this begin? When did this begin? I can't breathe. I can't—

"Marty? You okay, man?"

Allan's voice echoed from somewhere over the cube wall. There were other voices now, rising over the walls of the cubicle farm, but Marty couldn't see their faces. His vision was clouded with a swirling static, the frayed layers of reality peeling back at the edges, revealing an incomprehensible hell lurking just beneath. A hell of machinery and gears and appendages of flesh, every surface coated in slime and small pink worms and the coils of the tapeworms linked back to the membranous Gut at the heart of the facility. Somewhere above all the girders and wiring and tissue, a massive growth of eyes and teeth was latched on to the building, its tendrils hooked into every square inch of ██████████.

A terrible thought arced through his mind: *Is this how it starts? Is this how I'm to be promoted?* Marty could think of no other possibility. What he'd seen couldn't be unseen. Even as he struggled to regain his composure, his mind raced with the arcane knowledge afforded him by that glimpse between realities, and for the first time, he truly understood the madness of his customers.

His chest constricted, the need for air paramount but stifled by the suffocating mask on his face. In an act of desperation that would later become legend whispered in the halls of the company, Marty tore off his mask and let it clatter to the floor. His coworkers gasped at his action, but their curiosity and repulsion no longer concerned him. He sank to the floor, took a deep breath of stagnant air, and smiled with relief as consciousness gracefully slipped away from him.

11
THE MASKS WE WEAR

You're probably wondering what the big deal was about Marty taking off his smiler mask. I did tell you that people who get promoted don't have to wear them, but there's more to it than that. The Benefactors are big on the meaning and symbolism of ritual. There's power in someone's actions, especially when those actions run contrary to their nature, or when they come at a cost, and in the name of something far greater than themselves.

Taking off the mask is a sign of rebellion, a rejection of the reality with which we've all been blessed following the arrival of the Benefactors. Until we're promoted, we're all required to wear the masks. Not wearing it is a designation of rank—only if that rank has been granted. And while Marty Godot was beginning to experience the changes wrought by the promotion process, *he hadn't accepted the promotion yet.*

That's a big deal around here, friend. You're here by choice, even if this existence is hell. In here or out there, it's still your choice. ███████████ operates in an at-will state, and so does your existence. Whether he intended it to be or not, Marty's act of desperation was also one of defiance. The Acquisition marked the beginning of a new reality for mankind, and at great cost to the Benefactors. Acceptance of their ways and regulations is the least we can do to honor them and their continued benevolence. Were it not for them, we would have destroyed ourselves in the onslaught following the merger of realities.

Our masks exist to hide the truth from each other, however thinly veiled it might be, because we humans are fragile things. The Benefactors learned this the hard way. When a lowly software architect named Charles Boid built the Zer Zephanum web portal and communed with the Benefactors, pure chaos erupted through the office. Whole departments of employees were lost, mostly due to suicide, choosing to face oblivion rather than an eternity in immortal servitude.

Those who survived were driven mad by the truth in front of them. It's no secret the Benefactors exposed our base nature, revealing us to ourselves as the sophisticated animals we truly are. Sanity doesn't last when faced with the truth: that we're terrified creatures playing dress-up, pretending that we're safe, that everything's okay, and that life is something to be enjoyed. We need the illusion of happiness to survive.

The Benefactors turned a mirror on the human race, forcing us to see ourselves for the first time in our existence, and the truth was too much. The entire human race was drunk when the Benefactors arrived. The Acquisition forced sobriety on us all, and none of us could deal with it.

So, we wear the masks to feed the illusion, forcing a smile on all our faces while we manufacture a chemical to ease the burden of reality on everyone outside the company. We wear the masks to hide what the Benefactors are slowly doing to us in a physical sense. The tapeworm terminals will drain us into desiccated husks, beginning with our mouths, slowly eroding the soft flesh there, the lips, the gums. The cheeks deflate, the eyes bulge, the skin erupts in bubbling sores of blood and pus, and the hair begins to fall.

And we happy few, we keep right on smiling.

12
AT-WILL STATE

Marty awoke to soft candlelight and a low ululating hum. His head hurt, his eyes caked and crusty from dried blood, and when he sat up, he could not place his surroundings. The room was dim save for the candles affixed to sconces, the walls painted a dark red save for one side obscured in black drapery. His legs dangled in the air, forcing the realization that he was elevated off the ground, situated on a marble slab of ornate design.

Fragments of the hideous vision danced before his eyes, the phantoms of the void still haunting him in waking light, and he tried retracing what had happened. Marty remembered the nausea, the vomiting, the suffocating panic, the way the world peeled away from itself—and he remembered the mask.

Oh no.

A spike of fear drove its way into his gut when he realized the smiling façade was no longer affixed to his face. He lifted a trembling hand to his cheek, feeling his flesh for the first time in what might have been ages, tracing the lines in his skin around his mouth. His lips were shriveled, dry, his cheekbones a little too sharp, the skin stretched tightly like canvas.

The gravity of what he'd done pressed upon him, stealing the air from his lungs. *No mask, no smile, no job.*

No job.

That thought seemed oddly pleasant in the face of a promotion, something he'd tried so hard to avoid in his time at ███████████, however long that was. No job meant facing the agonizing madness beyond the walls of the company, but after what he'd glimpsed between the folds of reality, Marty supposed he could do no worse. An unsettling sensation trickled between the cracks of his mind, a steady drip of ice cold dread dropping right on the face of his resolve.

What if there's no difference? What if it doesn't matter?

The drapery ruffled, collapsing into itself as it was drawn outward, revealing a second room on the other side. A long table sat adjacent to the far wall, populated with seven figures clad in black robes, cowls, and white face masks. Behind them stood a pale wall of writhing flesh, pulsing with veins and oozing something like sweat from its pores, scarred with a lexicon of glyphs and cryptograms carved into the surface. Marty found he couldn't take his eyes off the symbols. He recognized some of them from his transcription work.

The central figure at the table gestured to him with a gloved hand. "Mr. Godot, thank you for meeting with us on such short notice. We hope you don't mind that you were brought to us. Time is short, and we couldn't wait. Glory be to Boid. Glory be to the Many."

"Glory be to Boid," Marty whispered, staring at the subtle glow of red light seeping from the open wounds on the wall. "Glory be to the Many."

Together, the panel of hooded figures removed their masks, revealing seven immaculate faces, seven pairs of eyes that glowed with the same shade of pale blue, and seven perfectly white smiles. He'd heard the stories of the drones in Human Resources, the way they were modeled after Saint Newmarth, albeit with a few choice modifications, but he'd never seen them unmasked before. The display of uniformity disturbed him, stirring a primal response in his gut to scream and flee.

A cluster of tapeworms uncoiled from below the marble slab, slithered upward, and latched onto his exposed skin just above his ankles. He wouldn't be going anywhere. They'd already seen to that.

"A good worker contributes to the company even during their downtime," one of them said. Its mouth didn't move. The sound of its voice squawked from a small black box affixed to its throat. "And you *are* a good worker, Mr. Godot. Aren't you?"

His manager's voice echoed in his mind. *You are proud, aren't you?* And he'd lied, the words coming to him so easily, a mistake he didn't want to make a second time.

Marty blinked, forced a smile. He tried to move his legs. The tapeworms remained in place, turgid as vines and just as tenacious, suckling away at the miserable blood coursing through him.

"Mr. Godot?"

"Yes," he said, lifting his stare to meet their faces. "I am a good worker."

"Which is why we've selected you for promotion, Mr. Godot. You've given so much to ███████████, and we feel it's time you gave even more."

Another HR representative spoke up: "Your record is nearly perfect."

"Nearly perfect," said another, its head bobbing up and down as though on a spring. "Your incident with your mask was unfortunate."

"Premature."

A recorded voice spoke in unison from their throat boxes: "Per Benefactor decree, section 12.39 of your Employee Manual, all ████████ employees of Tier 19 classification or lower must wear their company-issued smilers at all times while on the premises. Only in the event of an employee's promotion to Tier 20 or above will this decree be waived and superseded by section 15.83. If you have further questions, please consult the company intranet through the Zer Zephanum network portal."

The recording ended abruptly with a sharp hiss of static, followed by a litany of voices, all so similar that Marty had difficulty telling them apart.

"But certain infractions may be forgiven."

"All-Father Boid rewards the faithful. Glory be to Boid, glory be to the Many."

"Glory be to Boid. You have been most faithful, Mr. Godot."

"Most faithful."

"More transitions than any other employee in company history."

"Historic. Most impressive. Commendable."

"Your misery is most delicious when you are productive, and the Benefactors remain forever ravenous. Would you accept this promotion and ascend to a heightened level of servitude?"

A light above the table flickered to life, revealing a long blade with a hilt fashioned from bone. He hadn't noticed it before and wasn't certain it had been there at all until that moment. Below, the tapeworms released their hold, their suckered mouths freeing from his flesh with subtle pops. Warm blood trickled over his ankles and into his socks.

Confused, Marty hopped off the marble slab and slowly approached the table. The seven HR representatives watched him with frozen glee, their eyes and smiles locked upon him, and there they would remain for all eternity while awaiting his decision. As he neared, he saw thick tendrils of flesh coiled out from the wall, each one reaching toward the back of the representatives' chairs.

They're hooked in, he thought. *Part of the machine. Even they're being drained.*

The world shifted before him in that moment, another surge of static and mental electricity arcing across his fractured psyche. Reality lifted, peeling back to reveal more of the skeletal undercarriage of the building, the miles of tendrilled tapeworms coiled around the girders, connecting to the Gut, and back again with the massive membranous tumor on the roof. Everyone was connected at ███████████, each tier of employment beset with its own form of misery, and in that aspect all roles were the same. Promotion or no promotion, there was no difference. All were in bondage, serving the amorphous beast leeching life from the world.

"Mr. Godot?"

Marty blinked, and the world returned, but with that familiar red haze. He wiped the blood from his eyes. "Y-Yes, I'm—I'm just considering your offer. What are the benefits?" He paused, contemplating the absurdity of such a question. "*Are* there benefits?"

"Benefits." The representatives spoke this word in unison through widening smiles that nearly split their faces in half. They spoke apart from one another, following a script at random intervals, the glow in their eyes fading, distant.

"Of course there are benefits, Mr. Godot. ██████████ offers industry-competitive benefits, from a 401(k) contribution-matching program—"

"—to an annual incentive based on company performance. Accepting a promotion of this level will also afford you a corner office, a company credit card, a company-provided cellular phone—"

"—among other amenities. The promotion itself will afford you even more opportunities to serve the Benefactors—"

"—and you will become a vessel through which they will enact their will. One of the many—"

"—hands of the greater corporate entity, feeding the world with Euphoria™ as the Acquisition is finalized and the merger between realities is completed."

And finally, together: "Glory be to Boid, glory be to the Many."

The central representative offered its hand across the table. "Do you accept this offer of ascendance, Mr. Godot? Will you carve your name in the wall of reverence?"

"Do I have a choice?"

"You do, Mr. Godot. ██████████ operates in an at-will state. We may terminate your employment any time we wish—and so may you." Marty was about to speak his answer when the representative cut him off. "But know this, Mr. Godot. If you refuse this promotion, you will be effectively terminating your employment contract with ██████████, and all privileges granted to you within these walls will hereby be revoked. Do you understand?"

Marty considered his options, turning back to glance at the discarded smiler mask on the marble slab. He couldn't remember anything but his time at the company, and even those memories were subject to his mental dissonance. The thought of rising higher in the company and selling more of himself to the Benefactors turned his stomach. He'd already given so much, and to accept the promotion would mean giving even more. The alternative meant facing the madness beyond the walls of the Smile Factory, suffering between bouts of agonizing insanity while scrambling for the blissful ignorance of Euphoria™.

Immortality in servitude, or mortality in madness. The answer seemed obvious, and something happened to Marty in that moment. Something that he couldn't recall happening before, another memory stolen from him by his time at the company. The muscles in his face twitched, pulling upward into a pained smile.

"I do understand," he said, "and I've got one question for you."

The representatives smiled at him in silence. Behind them, the wall of flesh churned and shivered, its carved skin erupting in gooseflesh.

"Can you tell me how long I've worked here?"

The central representative retracted its hand and spoke without hesitation. "You have always worked for the company, Mr. Godot."

"Not anymore."

13

WE HAPPY FEW

I was there when they escorted him to the lobby. Two robed drones from HR brought him to the front desk. He had a box of personal items with him, which he sat on the front desk while the drones instructed me on what to do. See, until that point, no one had refused a promotion before. No one had ever opted out of their employment contract with the company. And I swear to you now, the look on that man's face was nothing but pure bliss.

When all was said and done, and Marty's badge was deactivated, the two HR drones said their farewells, wishing him a slow death in torment while the Benefactors robbed him of his sanity. When they were gone, he turned back toward the revolving glass doors and stared outside at the red sky and the unblinking eyes watching from the clouds. And then, you know what he did? He turned back to me, reached into his box of belongings, and handed me his smiler mask along with a pair of scissors.

"You need these more than I do," he said, pointing to the stitches in my lips. My manager had my lips sealed ages ago, said I couldn't keep my mouth shut. I took the scissors and cut the stitches. Even kept it a secret from my manager by hiding behind Marty's old smiler mask. I've been smiling for real all this time, and no one's been the wiser.

Marty Godot paid me that kindness in the moments before he walked out that door over there.

Yes, that one. If you look really hard, through all that swirling dust and fire out there, you can even make out his remains. Hate to say it, friend, but poor old Marty didn't last long out there. And good on him for that, you know? He went out on his own terms. He went out smiling for real while the rest of us can only wear our smiler masks and pretend.

That was the last time promotions were offered as a choice. Now they're mandated. Everyone Marty worked with—his boss, his coworkers—were promoted and never heard from again. Marty's name was stricken from the company records, the mention of him outlawed by management.

Why? Oh, well, isn't it obvious? He found a way to buck the system, friend. He figured out what they don't want us to know—that being in here is really no better than being out there. In some ways, it's worse, and now Marty's actions have rendered our contracts permanent—but hey, I don't hold anything against the man. Good on him for taking the initiative and facing a quick death instead of a slow eternity of rot.

Those of us here on the inside, the best we can hope for is to be devoured by the living thing within this facility and digested in the Gut, but that's never happened for as long as I've been here. The oldest of us are still here by the grace of All-Father Boid, our scarecrow bodies still pushing the buttons, pulling the levers, making the calls, and smiling.

Always smiling. Always happy.

Always living the illusion.

We happy few, enjoying the lie as it feeds our misery.

We happy few, allowing our misery to feed bliss to the world.

We happy few.

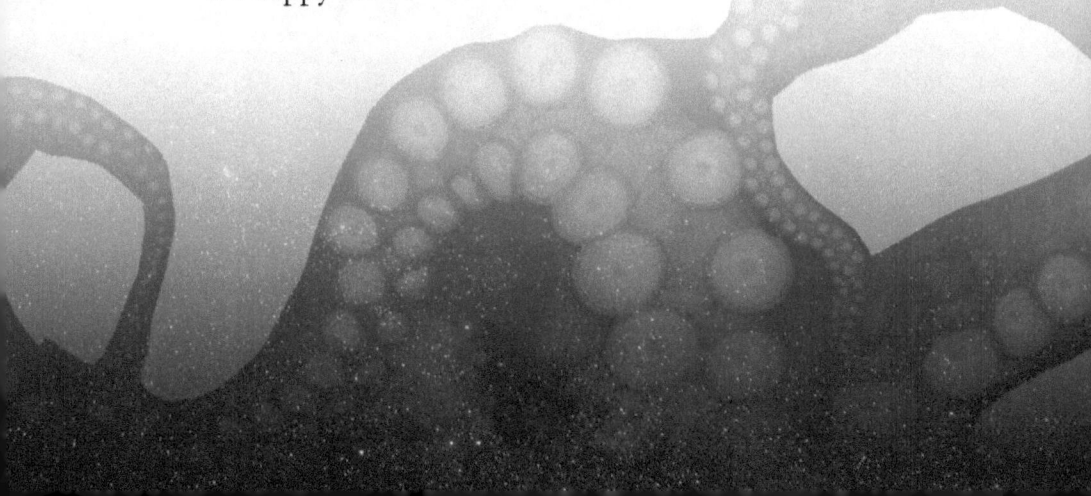

TODD KEISLING is the author of *A Life Transparent*, *The Liminal Man*, and the critically-acclaimed novella, *The Final Reconciliation*. His most recent release is the horror collection, *Ugly Little Things: Collected Horrors*, available now from Crystal Lake Publishing. He lives somewhere in the wilds of Pennsylvania with his family where he is at work on his next novel.

Share his dread:

Twitter: @todd_keisling
Instagram: @toddkeisling
www.toddkeisling.com

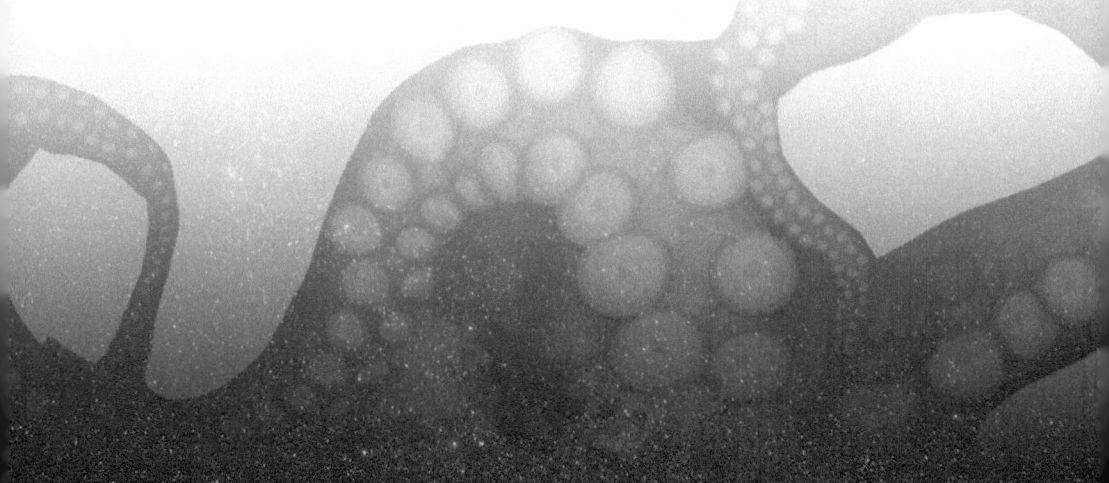